KING'S HARLOTS SERIES: BOOK 3

GRIM

J.M. WALKER

ISBN: 978-1-989782-05-7

ACKNOWLEDGEMENTS

Christine Stanley with The Hype PR. I can't even begin to tell you how much I appreciate you and all you have done for me. This series wouldn't be out there without your help.

Tammi Plummer. My wonderful PA. Girl, you are my #semicolon #BossPA. I can't thank you enough for your support and help in this never ending and amazing journey. We will make it to the top! I love you.

My beta readers. Jen Lum, Tammi Plummer and Angie Stanton. This book wouldn't be what it is today without your help. I love you girls.

To my Jems! You girls put up with my daily antics, my quirks, my random posts and more. You support me in everything and take a chance on my stories without even knowing what to expect. I can't thank you enough.

My review team and the Review Crew. I know this novella is a little different from the previous books but I can't thank you enough for taking a chance and reading it. For loving it. For supporting it. For hating it. All of your words have helped me grow.

All the bloggers, authors, readers, every single one of you who have shared, liked, commented, purchased the books from this series. I can't even begin to say how much you mean to me. How much I grow each day and am facsinated by that I'm in this book world. I learn so much from each and every one of you. You help me be a better writer. A better person.

I love each and every one of you. I wouldn't be where I am today if it weren't for you. Thank you. Just…

Thank you.

J.M. WALKER
XX

CHAPTER ONE

Jay

WITH ANGEL AT my side, anything was possible. We could conquer the world. As long as we were together, nothing would get in our way of being happy. Or so I thought. I couldn't focus on anything that was going on around me. So much shit had gone down that I fell deep within myself, and I didn't know how to get out.

Angel and I had been together for months, but nothing seemed right anymore. Our attraction to each other was fast and hard, our physical connection even more so. Once things died down with the human trafficking shit, we ended up in a rut. Or maybe it was just me. I couldn't be sure because Angel never said differently. I knew he loved me. He told me as often as he could. And he showed me even more. But I could still see he was hiding in that dark place he grew up in.

My thoughts were interrupted when Buck shifted his big furry weight against me. With his arm over my waist, he was almost as possessive as his owner.

"Sleep, princess," Angel murmured in my ear, wrapping himself over his dog and me.

Buck shifted, pushing him.

Angel chuckled, his deep laugh sending a shiver down my body. His breathing evened, his hold tight on my waist.

I sighed, scratching Buck's head.

These two were my life. Why these questions and thoughts were racing through my mind, I couldn't be sure. But it pissed me the fuck off.

I had always been a go getter. Embracing life to its fullest even though I was awkward and quiet. Losing my sister tore me in half, but it also made me stronger in the end. Now that she was home and safe, I should have been able to move on, but I didn't know how to.

Rolling over onto my side, I cupped Angel's cheek, brushing my thumb along his full bottom lip.

He was beautiful in a dark, demanding sort of way. Black scruff marred his strong jaw line, his bangs falling at the perfect angle along his forehead.

Buck jumped off the bed, curling himself into a ball in the corner of the room.

Angel shifted beside me.

Trailing my fingers down the line of his jaw, I moved them softly down the side of his neck to his strong shoulder. My thumb reached a scar on his pec, brushing over it slightly.

Angel's eyes fluttered open, darkening to a point where all I could focus on was him. Us. It had always been him and me. Angel and Jay. King and Queen.

Before I knew what was happening, he had me under him and his hips between my legs. "What's wrong?" he asked, kissing the soft spot under my ear at the same time he pushed his pelvis into me.

I groaned, wrapping my hands around the back of his neck. "Nothing."

"Don't lie to me," he growled, nipping his teeth into my skin.

I jumped, arching beneath him. No matter how many times we had been together, it was still as intense as the first time.

"I'm not," I panted, my body becoming alive at his touch. It had always been like that. One touch and I was done. I was his. He made me feel like the most important person in the world. That it was just him and me.

"Jay," Angel whispered, trailing kisses along my jawline. He sunk his teeth into my bottom lip before forcing his tongue into my mouth. Every time he kissed me, he breathed new life into my lungs. Releasing me with a wet smack, he licked his tongue along my bottom lip.

A shiver shot straight down my back, hitting me in the center of my fucking soul.

"You're lying." He sat back on his haunches, kneading his fingers into the flesh of my thighs.

"What do you want from me, Angel?" Desire simmered as frustration took over. I didn't know how to answer his questions. Now that there was nothing to distract us, we had been fighting more. I couldn't remember how it started. Nightmare after nightmare of my past forced old feelings to the surface. The dark evil that had taken over my life as a young girl. The desire to hurt and the pain it caused.

"I want you to tell me what's going on. Why have we been fighting?" Angel gripped my hips. Although he was hard and ready for me, he didn't do anything about it.

Licking my lips, my fingers itched to reach out to him. To grab hold of his powerful body, knowing he would give me everything I desired. He would take away the terror of my past. He had already started. But what would he think if I told him I was still scared? That every night I woke up in a cold sweat because the fingers of death had visited me only moments before. That all of the monsters who had destroyed a piece of this town deserved to die.

"You're not going to tell me, are you?" Angel's mouth set in a firm line, his jaw clenching. "If we want this to move forward, we need to be honest and open with each other. I fucking proposed to you, Jay."

My heart thumped. I remembered his unconventional proposal. He had told me he wanted to spend the rest of his life with me. And I told him that I felt the same way. It wasn't anything fancy. It was perfect. It was us, and it was ours. I wouldn't have asked for it to be any other way.

"I'm not a talker, but yet here I am, talking," Angel huffed, rubbing the back of his neck. His dark gaze peered down at me. "Why are you shutting me out?"

I swallowed hard, the dry lump in my throat burning. "I don't know what to say."

"Be honest with me." He cupped my cheek, placing a soft peck on my mouth. "That's all I can ask for."

Tilting my head, I returned the kiss and wrapped my hands around his neck.

"What are you so scared of?" he whispered against my lips.

Us.

***

Scars embedded on my soul.

The physical pain was nothing like the mental anguish that had been inflicted on me over the past couple of months. What did I do to deserve this?

My sister would be so disappointed in me.

Tyler Bone was the bad boy of Dante's Kings. Becoming the new prospect in my daddy's motorcycle club, I would fall all over myself to get his attention. And when I did, hell swallowed me whole.

"Jenny, grab me a fucking beer." Tyler's deep voice rumbled through me, punching me in the heart that I had been so willing to give him. He had all of me. Every single piece. But I didn't know how to take any of it back.

"Jenny!" he boomed.

I jumped from my spot on the floor where he had beat me down. The pain in my ribs made it hard to breathe, but I refused to show him how bad he had hurt me.

It had been that way since Tyler got what he wanted and made Vice President. My father trusted him. And I looked good on his arm, so he kept me by his side.

Grabbing a beer from the fridge, I made my way to the bastard as fast as I could.

"It's about time." He snatched the bottle from my hand, peering up at me through dark eyes. "On your knees."

My heart jumped. "Tyler."

"I don't suggest making me repeat myself," he said, his voice calm and even.

Lowering to the floor, I wiped my sweaty palms on my pants.

Safe place, Jay. Safe place. You got this. You're strong. You will make it out.

"My beautiful Jenny." Tyler leaned forward, pinching my jaw, and forced me to look up at him. "If you only cooperated, it would never have to be like this."

"Yes, it would."

He smirked. "You know me too well.

For the next hour, he did whatever he wanted to me and took it without remorse. He forced me to submit in ways that should never be allowed.

Even though this had only been going on for a couple of months, the abuse had been happening since the first time I saw him. I just never knew it then.

"I love you, Jenny," Tyler whispered to me later that evening. "You know you like it when I hurt you."

I turned to him, my gaze roaming down his bare chest. His tanned skin was marred by my violent touch.

Bile rose to my throat.

Looking up at the ceiling, I vowed at that point never to trust again. And if this is what love was, I didn't want it.

***

(Angel)

Being taken by Vega destroyed a part of Jay that I wasn't sure how to get back for her. Maybe that piece of her was gone for good. He forced her to choose life over death and watch girls kill themselves. But they never died. It was a complete mind-fuck, and it did what he wanted it to do.

Eric Vega fucked Jay up.

She was closed off, snapping at anyone who was around to hear it. The world had tilted on its axis, bringing us together. As soon as we were happy, a wedge was driven between us.

Girls were still missing. Jay's sister had finally been found. Was that it? Did Jay's estranged relationship with her twin, Violet, put this fear in her?

Jay wouldn't talk to me about it, and that pissed me the fuck off. We had been through a lot together. I would die for the woman laying beneath me. She taught me to love. She opened up something inside of me that had been closed off for years. And now she was doing the same.

"You need to talk to me," I told her, running my fingers down her cheek. With a raging hard-on between my legs, I breathed through the impending urge to just fuck her and be done with it.

She met my stare, a questioning look in her gaze before she reached out for me. Her hand wrapped around my cock, stroking from base to tip.

I hissed out a breath, my head falling back on my shoulders. "Fuck." Her hands felt so fucking good. I could never get enough. Jay was my addiction. She was the pure heroin I had heard about. The ultimate high that druggies craved. And she was mine.

With her hand working my dick, all I could do was kneel there. My hands found her hips, gripping tight until my fingers dug into her flesh.

"You like that, baby?" she purred.

"You're ... distracting ... me," I panted, rolling my hips in tune with her hand.

"Your cock is delicious." She shrugged. "It's not my fault it wanted to come out and play."

"Geeze, woman." Pulling from her grip, I flipped her onto her stomach.

She let out a soft gasp, arching beneath me.

"Just because you're teasing me—" I thrust inside of her "—doesn't mean I won't get the answers I'm looking for."

Jay pushed her ass against me, matching my movements. "Just fuck me, Angel. That's all I'm giving you right now."

Fuck, this woman and what she did to me. I couldn't control it. Her touch. Her demands. Everything about her brought me to my knees. She was the ultimate undoing to my control. I loved her. With every single inch of me. I knew her inside and out, but when she shut down on me, it forced the ugly part of myself to come out and play.

Digging my fingers into the flesh of her ass, I lifted her and pushed her head into the pillow. She wouldn't give me the answers I needed? Fine. I would fuck her however I felt. I was pissed. And I made sure to let her know it.

"Angel," she cried out, shaking beneath me.

My girl liked it rough and dirty, and I made sure to show her exactly how rough I could be. My thrusts powered into her. My fingers dug into her pale skin. I gripped her hair, pulling her upright, and wrapped a hand around her slender throat.

"You think just because you can tease me with your beautiful body and soft demands that I won't get the answers I'm looking for?" I growled, sinking my teeth into the soft spot beneath her ear.

She moaned, shivering against me. "I know you can't resist me."

My blood thundered in my ears. As much as I didn't want to, as much as my cock wanted me to give in, I released her.

Jumping off the bed, I pulled on my pants, the cotton rubbing over the strained erection.

"What the hell do you think you're doing?" she snapped, her eyes heating with fire.

I chuckled, cupping myself. "You want my dick? Tell me what the *fuck* is going on."

Jay glared. She took deep breaths before she turned over onto her back. "Fine. You won't fuck me? I'll just continue myself." Her hand reached between her legs, her fingers flicking over her swollen clit.

My dick jumped. *Fuck.* She played nasty.

She whimpered, letting me hear all of the sounds I craved. "Angel, baby." She arched beneath her touch, her finger slipping inside her center. "Please."

"Are you begging me?" I breathed, not able to take my eyes off her hand.

"No." Her finger thrust in and out of her glistening pussy. "*You're* going to beg *me*." Her hand moved from between her legs to her mouth. The finger that had just been inside of her body now inches away from her lips.

My cock swelled, pre-cum dripping off the end. Fuck. I couldn't handle it. She wouldn't dare.

Peeking her tongue out, she licked along her finger, a soft moan escaping the back of her throat. "I taste good, Angel." Her eyes were dark and wild, demanding that I do what I did best. Her lips closed around her finger, and that was when I lost it.

She knew my weakness. The fact that her taste was on her lips sent a shiver racing up my spine and controlled my next actions before I could comprehend what I was doing.

Grabbing her ankles roughly, I pulled her off the bed and into my arms before she could scream out my name.

I spun her, ripped down my pants, and drove into her so hard I had her coming undone in seconds. My name left her mouth on a guttural cry. Her hips slammed into mine, her hot cunt sucking me dry until I couldn't give anymore.

A half an hour later, we fell to the floor, with my dick still inside of her, ready to go again.

This. This was what I lived for. Every damn day of my life.

"I told you you couldn't resist me." She stifled a yawn, curling into me.

I didn't say anything. I only watched and cared for her. With my marks on her body and my come inside of her, my love for her went deeper.

She would tell me what was going on. Whether she liked it or not.

CHAPTER TWO

Jay

"YOU'RE BEAUTIFUL."

"I hate you."

"You love me."

"No, I don't."

Tyler smirked. "Yes, you do, or else you still wouldn't be here. In my bed. Filled with my come."

A year ago, I would have cried, bawling like a baby over the pain he had caused me.

But now, on this cool summer evening, I laid with the man who destroyed the innocent part of my soul.

He was right.

I did love him but not in the way one should. I loved him because he fed the dark part of my soul. Since Violet was taken *from me, he was all I knew. He allowed me to unleash my anger on him. Hitting him until I was spent and sore.*

Tyler was the only person who believed that Violet was taken. That she wouldn't just walk off with some random guy and not tell me about it. My own father didn't believe that she was a victim. She had always been the wild one. While she was gone, I took over that role. My timidness no longer a factor in this game called life.

"Why do you hit me?" I finally asked, breaking the unnerving silence that I had become accustomed to.

"Why do you hit me back?" Tyler rose from the bed, pulled on his torn jeans, and turned to me. His dark hair had become long in the past couple of months. So long he had to put it back into a ponytail.

"I hit you back because …" I sat up, swallowing past the disgust of his semen leaking from my body. "It's all I know."

"Well, my dear Jenny. There's your answer."

I frowned. "What the hell does that mean?"

He raised an eyebrow. "Careful. I don't care if you're all used up."

I looked away. Sliding my legs over the edge of the bed, I sat there, staring at myself in the reflection of the mirror. I had become pale. Skinny to the point you could see my ribs poking out of my skin. But no one noticed.

"Do you like what you see?" Tyler crawled onto the bed behind me, wrapping his large hand around my slender throat. "I like seeing how red I can make your skin. And I know you enjoy digging your nails into mine."

"I hate you," was all I said.

"Fuel that hate, Jenny. One day you will need it."

Tyler had been right. He had said those words so many years before, but I never thought anything of it.

Angel wanted answers.

I knew I needed to tell him what was going on with me. But I had no idea where to start. How do you tell your current boyfriend that your ex still comes to you in your nightmares?

My body shivered at the constant memories of Tyler beating me, yelling at me, and forcing me to do whatever he desired. It was funny, though, because in the end, I didn't put up much of a fight. I ended up enjoying it. It was sick and twisted how I would egg him on to the point of no control. It was why I did it with Angel. I couldn't help it. I craved his force. He would never hurt me. Not unless I needed him to. In a masochistic kind of way, I savored when he spanked me and dug his fingers into my flesh.

Buck sniffed at my feet, lifted his head, looked around, and let it drop back down on his outstretched paws.

My toes scratched at his fur, gently petting him. He had been the one thing that kept me calm. With Angel, I loved him with all of me, but he was intense. His love for me was like a living breathing thing. I could *feel* him before he even walked into a room.

As if Buck could sense my thoughts, he rose from his spot on the floor and moved to the empty space beside me. Angel didn't like him being on the couch, but I didn't care. I enjoyed having Buck's head in my lap while I drank my morning coffee.

After everything with Eric Vega, I fell into myself. The man destroyed a part of me I never knew was there. Since my sister was taken, I became hard, cold. But Angel melted that ice and showed me that I could be filled with warmth again.

We never talked about Vega and his part in the human trafficking. He took me. Shot himself. Angel saved me. And that was it. But we needed to talk about it—it was eating us both alive like a deadly virus.

Shadows of memories threatened to consume me, and if I wasn't careful, they would swallow me whole.

Angel did what he could to bring me away from the darkness.

The hospital had offered counseling. The Navy had offered Angel the same thing, and he asked if I wanted to go. I had told him he was all I needed. But I wasn't even sure if that were true anymore. Maybe talking to someone *would* help.

"What are you doing, princess?" Angel asked, peering his head out the patio door.

"Just hanging out with Buck." I scratched his ears, smiling when he let out a heavy sigh.

Angel nodded. "Okay. Well, I have to head into town. Are you coming with me?"

I moved to stand when I could feel the blood draining from my head. "Oh …" I wavered on my feet.

"Jay?" Angel rushed to my side. "Are you okay?"

"I … Yes. Just light headed. I haven't eaten much today."

Angel pinched my chin, forcing me to look up at him. "Are you sure?"

"I am." I smiled for added measure. "I'll go into town with you."

"Okay." He grabbed my hand, leading me back into his house. He called for Buck, the old dog following soon after. "We need to talk about earlier," Angel told me while grabbing his keys.

"I know."

Walking hand in hand to his big black SUV, he opened the door for me.

I smiled up at him and climbed into the vehicle.

It was funny thinking how in the beginning, I expected to do everything myself. Doors being opened. Bills being paid while on a date …

"We've never gone on a date," I told Angel when he slipped into the SUV beside me.

"What?"

"A date," I repeated. "We've never been on one."

"Well, it's been kind of hard with all of the shit going on." He started the vehicle, pulling out of the long driveway and spoke again when he reached the road. "Are you wanting to go on a date?"

"Yeah. No. Maybe?" I rung my hands in my lap, my cheeks burning.

He slowed to a stop, gently taking my chin, and turned my face toward him. "Jay, if you want to go on a date, you don't have to ask. It's kind of a given that we're dating." He reached for my hand. "I love you, princess. I hope you know that."

Curling my fingers in his, I brushed my thumb over the tiny scars on his knuckles. So much pain. So many tears and heartache. To think I almost pushed him away completely in the beginning. I thanked God that Angel was stubborn and wouldn't give up on me. *On us.*

"If you would like to go on a date, we can." He pulled me closer, wrapping his arm around my shoulders.

"I would like that," I mumbled against his sweater.

"I would like that too." He kissed my knuckles. "Don't give up on us."

My eyes snapped up to his. "I'm not."

"Promise?"

"Yes."

GRIM

***

(Angel)

With my eyes on the road, I still noticed the darkness in Jay's eyes. Vega had stolen that light from her. The light I had fallen in love with. Because of that bastard, I lost a part of my girlfriend, and it terrified the shit out of me that I would never get it back. Counseling only did so much, and Jay and I were the same when it came to talking to strangers. We couldn't even talk to each other, let alone some random person. They didn't know us. They wouldn't know how to fix whatever shit was going on. Jay and I would have to work through this together.

In time.

Time was all we had. There were moments where it felt like it was *all* we had. Too much. Not enough. There was never a happy medium.

"Angel?"

"Yeah, baby?" I kissed her head, breathing in the scent of her vanilla body wash.

"I love you." She smiled up at me. "I do. Please know that."

"Of course I do." I turned to her when I pulled into the parking lot and shut off the engine. "Why would you think I wouldn't?"

"Because …" She shrugged. "I know we need to talk about everything, but I'm not ready. I need you to have patience. And … I know I'm difficult."

"Jay, I knew you were difficult the first time you told me to go to hell. I fell in love with you right then and there. You forced your way into my heart, and I'm never letting you go." I cupped her cheek. "Know *that.*"

Her chin trembled, her eyes glassing over.

Fuck. This was unlike her. Jay didn't cry over anything. "I will try and have patience. I will. But I need you to understand that we have to talk." *Fuck.* Even I didn't like those words leaving my mouth, but I wasn't stupid. Communication was key. "I love you, princess. I don't tell you that enough."

Pulling away from me, she slid out of the vehicle and stretched her arms above her head.

I quickly did the same, coming up behind her, and wrapped myself around her middle. Brushing my nose into the crook of her neck, I snarled.

She giggled, leaning into me.

That sound. It sent a hot shiver straight to my balls. I lived for her laughter.

"Thank you." Jay turned toward me, hugging her arms around my waist. "I love you, Angel."

The only response I had was to kiss her fully on the mouth. No words were said. They weren't needed. I made a promise with myself at that point that I would show her just how much she meant to me and how much I loved her. We would get through this shit with Violet, Tyler, every fucking problem … together.

CHAPTER THREE

Jay

THE LAUGHTER THAT left my body was fake. Masked by happiness when really my chest was filled with so much hate, it squeezed and tugged at my soul. The vile men who threatened to destroy our small town would die. I would make sure of it. This anger was fueled by the fucked-up world we lived in.

When Angel and I had walked into the clubhouse, that angry darkness inside of me grew when I saw Meeka sitting at a booth by herself. Something unleashed inside of me back when Vega had kidnapped me. Maybe it had been there all along.

Everything in me told me to go to Meeka. To scream and yell, demand to know why she did what she did. I knew. Her words repeated over and over again in mind.

"I had to."

She kept my sister from me and used me as bait. The anger tore at my soul, threatening to consume me.

"It's over and done with, Jay," Angel whispered in my ear. "Let it go."

I bit back a scoff. He meant well but right then, I didn't want to let it go. It wasn't possible. And this hate I felt only made me stronger. It would help me battle the impending war whenever Charles Brian decided to show himself again.

Asher Donovan had been the other part of that whole operation. Angel's brother. A man he had gone to hell and back with. It destroyed a piece of him. He had only just begun to learn how to love, how to open himself up to these new feelings, and then he found out his brother had been keeping this secret the whole time.

"Hi, Meeka," I blurted.

Her eyes snapped up from her phone. "Hi," she muttered. She moved to get up from the booth but hesitated.

"We have a meeting at five," I told her. "But you and I are meeting beforehand."

She nodded. "Okay."

"Good girl," Angel mumbled in my ear. "It's about time you retract those claws of yours."

"Fuck off, Angel."

He wrapped his arm around my shoulders and kissed me fully on the mouth. "So much fucking sass."

I breathed him in. Every sense of him. His taste washed over me, making my heart skip several beats before I had to come up for air. One kiss and I was done. A second kiss and I would be falling to my knees at his feet, begging like a bitch in heat.

"It makes me hard knowing my kiss turns you on to the point of no control," he purred, kissing my neck.

I shivered, grabbing his hand, and led him to my room at the back of the club. I needed him to show me I could feel something besides this dread and worry.

"Jay," he ground out, closing the door behind him.

I turned toward him, stripping out of my clothes. "I need you to fuck me." Sex wasn't an out. It wasn't an excuse to ignore our problems but right then, it was all I wanted.

"Kneel." Angel came toward me, unbuckling his belt. "I'm going to fuck that pretty mouth of yours for being so demanding."

I lowered to the floor, tilting my head back. I waited. For him. For that control I had but didn't want.

For the next hour or so, Angel unleashed something inside of me. He took control, dominated my body, and stole my heart. I loved him. Every inch of him. But that nagging feeling of whether he would hurt me or not kept poking me.

"No man will ever love you the way I do," Tyler said, his deep voice whispering across my skin. "And you will never open up again. You are mine forever, Jenny, whether you like it or not."

He was right. With his bruises on my flesh, scars on my heart, and his body inside of mine, the only choice I had was to submit. There was no other way. No out. I was trapped like a rat in a cage. Clawing and scratching until my fingers bled.

The vile man fucking me forced me to look at him. The names he called me.

Slut. Whore. Bitch. Slave.

He loved me.

GRIM

My mind played tricks on me. Falling in and out of the darkness that I begged to consume me.

A hard slap landed against my cheek.

The sting should have brought tears to my eyes. The burning sensation of where his palm hit should have caused me to cry out. But it didn't. It had come to this, hadn't it? He hit. I submitted. He forced me to do things I never would have thought possible. And after a while, I found myself craving them. Him. Tyler Bone.

"I love you, princess," Angel's words whispered across my skin, followed by his hand sliding down my side to my hip. "I will show you. With every breath, every inch, every ounce of me that I love you."

I floated in and out of sleep, listening to his words. Holding onto them like they were the life line I needed to make it through each day.

Memories of Tyler and our dangerous relationship repeated themselves every time I closed my eyes. I thought I loved him, but Angel showed me what true love was.

Our love had been strong, growing intense as each day passed. With him lying beside me, his deep breathing evening out as his peaceful dreams took over, I couldn't help but wonder if this was real. If it was just a dream. With a click of my heels, this fantasy would end, and I would be forced to go back to a time where abuse was all I knew.

"Whatever happens, I am here," Angel told me while we were lying in each other's arms.

"I don't want anything to happen," I mumbled, curling into him, grazing my hand down his bare chest.

"I know, baby." He kissed my temple, letting his lips linger when his phone rang. He answered it, and I zoned out.

All this time, I thought Vega had destroyed that tiny bit of strength left that I had. But I realized that it had been Tyler all along. He promised me that I would never find love again with another man. I did, but the fear of Angel hurting me burned its way into my heart. It was what Tyler wanted.

"I'm with Jay," Angel told the caller.

At the mention of my name, I looked his way.

He pinched the bridge of his nose which I had come to know was his signature move whenever he was stressed. "We need her in, Asher."

Meeka. My stomach twisted.

"Well, of course she's not going to agree easily." Angel sat up straighter. "It's not like you're giving her a choice … I told you to get someone you trust. I assumed it would be her but do not blame this shit on me. Fine … I know … I love you too, brother." Angel threw the phone on the end table.

"What the hell's going on?" I asked, a sliver of annoyance rushing through my body.

Angel cupped my nape, capturing my mouth in a hard bruising kiss before leaning his forehead against mine. "I can't tell you everything yet."

"It's work related," I finished for him. "But why does it have to do with Meeka?"

"I'll explain when I can." *Or when he would have no choice* went unsaid. "Please trust me." He kissed my nose.

I pushed out of his embrace. "Of course I trust you, but I'm fucking sick of these secrets. Tell me what's going on."

"I can't. You know that."

"Fine. Don't tell me," I grumbled. "See if I fucking care."

"What the hell is this, Jay?" He frowned. "You know I can't tell you anything when it comes to my fucking job."

"I know that," I snapped. "But these girls are my sisters. When it comes to them, you have to tell me."

"No, I don't."

"Why the hell not?" I threw back at him. "What does Meeka have to do with this?" Not that I overly cared but if what she was involved in effected my other sisters, I would throw her to the wolves and leave her there to rot.

"You need to trust me," he repeated, shoving a hand roughly through his hair.

"And you need to tell me what is going on."

He reached for me, grabbing my hand, and pulled me against him.

"Angel," I attempted to push out of his grip. "Talk to me."

"Asher is needing Meeka's help. That's all I can say for now." Angel ran his hands down my back. "What are you doing before the meeting today?"

"Stop trying to change the subject," I mumbled.

He chuckled, kissing my forehead.

"I hate you right now."

"No, you don't."

He was right. I didn't. But he sure as fuck pissed me the hell off. "I need to hit the shop," I said, finally answering his question. "I have a couple interviews to set up at some point as well." Tattooed had been my dream. It was a new business, with me being the only tattoo artist until now. Creena Chan, King's Harlots newest prospect, kept things in order for me and did what she could. Business was booming for both of us but I needed someone to man the cash and make sure Tattooed didn't go under.

"Dale said he was working on the new sign for you." Angel rose from the bed and pulled on his jeans.

"Yeah, but he doesn't listen well. I told him I wanted classy but bold. He tried showing me flashing signs and wanted to add sparklers at one point."

Angel laughed. "That's my brother."

I smiled, getting dressed as well. "He means well, I guess."

"I'm glad you're getting along with them." Angel closed the distance between us and grabbed both of my hands. "It means everything to me that they accept you and take you in. If something happened to me, I need to know that you're protected."

"Nothing is going to happen to you. To either of us. No one is getting fucking taken again." I pulled out of his grip and shoved my top over my head. "No one."

***

(Angel)

"No one."

Jay's words. Desperate and driven by fear and hate.

My chest panged that I couldn't take that away from her. My soul cried out with the need to make her feel better. Even for just a little bit. I poured those pleas to help her into our love making. I tried so hard with everything in me to let her feel my love for her. I didn't say it enough. She inspired me. She was a powerful woman in a fucked-up man's world but she didn't give up. She made it so other women wanted to follow suit.

"I don't want to go to this meeting," Jay muttered a couple hours later. It was supposed to have been at the club, but Asher had asked for us to show up at his place. So we were all on our way, much to my fiancé's disapproval.

"I know you and Meeka need to work through your shit, but we all need to be together on this," I told her, kissing her knuckles before letting them drop in her lap. "I need you in on this with me."

"Why do I have to go? I deal with this shit much better at the club."

That sentence bothered me. She didn't say it was *her* club, and it hadn't been the first time. "Jay."

She sighed, her shoulders slumping but she wouldn't meet my gaze.

"Jay," I repeated, my voice firm.

She huffed but finally looked my way.

Vega messed with her head. And it destroyed me more than her. When she was taken, I lost a part of myself. We both did. Somehow, she came out stronger in the end, and I was the one who became weak.

I pulled her into my arms, cradling her head against my chest.

Her back stiffened.

Holding her at arm's length, I searched her face.

When she raised an eyebrow, the hint of emotion that was there seconds before disappeared when the darkness took over.

Jay pushed out of my hold.

Giving her the space she needed, I stood back and watched her. But it would be over my dead body before I ever let her deal with this shit on her own.

CHAPTER FOUR

Jay

YOU WOULD THINK after getting my sister back, I would spend every chance I could with her. That I would make sure she was safe or have someone watching her every hour of every day. But I didn't. Something had changed in her. She became hard, falling into herself until she was trapped. She never talked about what happened during the years she was missing. A part of me didn't want to know the torture she went through for fear that I would turn into the mere monster we were chasing.

Violet and I chatted on the phone as often as possible. Texted, emailed, and so on. But things had been uncomfortable. I blamed myself for her disappearance. I knew the only people to blame were the ones who took her, but I should have been there for her. I should have been there like Tyler was there for me. It was the only thing I had been truly thankful for when it came to him.

"Tyler," I cried, falling against him. "My sister ... Violet ..."

"What happened?" he asked, cupping my cheeks. "Tell me."

"She's ... she's missing," I sobbed, no longer having the strength to hold back my tears.

"What do you mean she's missing?"

Memories of that God awful day would always have a permanent place on my heart. Tyler was an abusive asshole, but he was also the only person who believed me.

As if she could hear my thoughts, Violet's picture showed up on my phone. It had been on silent but having that twin vibe, I didn't need it to ring to know when she would call.

"Hey," I answered.

Angel took that as his cue to leave the SUV and walk around to my door. Opening it, he reached for my hand.

I had almost forgot that I wasn't alone. Sliding my fingers in his, I let him pull me from the vehicle.

"Hey yourself," Violet said softly.

"How are you?" It was the same conversation we had every single day. Small talk. Forced questions. It became robotic and scripted.

"Good," she answered automatically. "How are you?"

"Good," I repeated. Violet had been brought back to me. It had been weeks since her safe return, but a part of her was still missing. "Listen, Violet. We … I …"

"I know," she whispered. "I'm selling my house."

Well, that was new. "You are? Why?"

"Too many bad memories. My therapist suggested it. It's to help me start over."

"What about the apartment?" She had been staying at my place for the past couple of weeks.

"That's what I wanted to talk to you about." Her breath hitched. "I'm thinking of renting my own place. I found this cute loft that's affordable. I just … I need to start over."

"I understand that but the security Dad set up will keep you safe."

"I'm fine."

"Well, I'm not," I snapped. "I need to know that you're safe. I lost you for years. I thought you were fucking dead."

"Jay," her voice shook. "I'm sorry."

"Don't be sorry." My hand tightened on the phone. "Just don't make any rash decisions. Let's talk about this first," I suggested, my heart jumping.

"Okay," she paused. "I *am* sorry."

"I know, Violet. Life has fucking sucked these past couple of years, and I need you to be happy," I said as my throat burned. "I need my sister back, but I also need to know that you're safe."

"I know."

It was a given that things would be different. She had been taken from me, from us, for years.

We said our goodbyes, and all I could do was stare at the phone in my hand.

"Are you okay, princess?" Angel wrapped his arms around my shoulders.

"No," I whispered. But I refused to cry. I was sick of this shit. I would help Violet find herself again. I would get back my sister, and I would put an end to the motherfuckers who threatened to destroy the lives of innocent girls.

"You *will* get through this." He cupped my jaw, brushing his thumb over my bottom lip. "I promise you. And I will be here every step of the way."

I wasn't a woman who depended on a man. I never had been and never would be. But with Angel by my side, I felt like the strongest person ever and that I could take on the whole fucking world. He didn't complete me. He *complemented* me. We were strong apart but even more powerful when we were together.

"Remember who you are," he told me, brushing his mouth over mine. "You're Genevieve Gold, and you're the strongest woman I know. I don't tell you that often. You inspire me, Jay. To be a better man. To be a better fucking person. I wouldn't be where I am if it wasn't for you."

His sweet words slid over my skin, piercing me straight in the heart and forcing it to skip several beats. "I'm not strong," I admitted.

There was a battle raging inside of me. So many things needed to be said. I wanted to rip off Meeka's head for keeping Violet from me and for using me as fucking bait. I got in her face once, but it wasn't enough. She didn't fight me. I wanted her to fight me. I wanted her to yell back that it was needed. That all of this shit was needed. That there was a reason for all of our mistakes. I needed to hit something. "Angel."

"Yeah, princess?"

"Let's get this meeting over with. I need to hit something, and I need you."

He kissed my head. "You have me. Whatever happens, you will always have me, and I will give you anything that you need."

Angel loved me. I knew he felt guilty for not telling me often how he felt about me but I didn't need him to say the words. He showed it, and that was enough for me.

He never knew how to love, and now that something had been opened up inside of him, he couldn't stop the words from leaving his mouth every chance he could.

When we stepped into Asher's house, I wasn't sure what to expect. Meeka was standing with him, talking amongst themselves. He glanced at her with affection in his eyes. Her cheeks would redden. There was something there, and they didn't even know it yet.

"You need to talk to her, princess." Angel brushed his hand down my back. "Before it's too late."

"It's already too late," I mumbled, crossing my arms under my chest.

"You know you want to talk to her."

"What am I supposed to say, Angel? Should I tell her how mad I am? She already knows that. Should I tell her that I want to forgive her but I can't?"

"You will forgive her," Angel said gently. "You just need time. I know you two have never been close, but I also know that you need her. Just like you need the other girls."

I huffed. "Why do you always have to be right?"

He chuckled, kissing my head. "I don't expect you to forget or even to forgive right away but it's been weeks since Violet was brought back to you."

"They used me as bait, Angel. Aren't you pissed over that?"

GRIM

His jaw clenched. "You have no fucking idea."

***

(Angel)

I knew Asher meant well. I knew the situation involving the girls forced everyone to become desperate. We were all driven with the need to save them, and we all had our own personal reasons as to why.

There was a force behind this operation and whether it was human or the business itself was yet to be determined. Either way, we would end it.

We had been looking into who was the front runner, the leader, the fucking Master of this shit but all roads led to nothing. Nada. Zip. Zilch. It was beyond frustrating, and it was putting a wedge in our group. Of course, Vice-One brushed it off like it was nothing but our eyes told all. Especially Coby's. My brother had been through shit, seen shit, and lived to *not* talk about it. He was a vault.

The fact that Asher, a man I trusted, took the woman I loved to bring home her sister forced a rage inside of me I had never felt before. It was consuming, and if I didn't unleash it soon, it would take over. I knew it. *He* knew it. Every time he looked at me, I could see the questioning glance of if I would hit him or not. I wanted to. I wanted to drive my fist into his face and demand for him to tell me what the hell he was thinking. But instead, I told him to go undercover to bring Charles Brian down. And I convinced him to bring Meeka into it as well. What did that say about me? I was an asshole. I lived up to that name, but at that moment, I didn't care.

"What are you thinking about, Angel?" Jay asked, raising an eyebrow. She wrapped her arms around my waist and kissed my cheek.

"I'm thinking about how much I love you." I brushed my mouth along hers, igniting a soft purr to leave her lips.

"Funny." She pulled back. "Too bad I know you and know that you were thinking about this … about everything."

"We'll talk later." Because in all honesty, I didn't want to discuss our shit in front of our friends. I didn't want anyone knowing that there was a problem. That I was so pissed off I forced my brother into this mess.

"Sorry to interrupt," Meeka said, approaching us. "Can I talk to you for a second, Jay?"

"No." Jay frowned, turning back to me.

"What the hell was that?" I demanded, my brows narrowing.

"I'm not ready," Jay cried.

"Meeka," Asher grit out, leaning against the wall. "Come here, hummingbird." He reached a hand out to her.

She walked into his outstretched arms, curling against him.

They talked amongst themselves, with Asher consoling his best friend.

"What was that, Jay?" I asked, lowering my voice so only she could hear.

"What, Angel? What do you want me to do?" Her eyes darkened. "I'm not ready. I don't know if I'll ever be ready."

"You need time," I reminded her, earning a hard glare. I chuckled, cupping her nape, and pulled her against me.

GRIM

She sighed. "How come I can't stay mad at you? You say shit that gets on my nerves because I know you're right but yet … I'm happy."

"I don't know …" I kissed her head. "Maybe it's because we're in love. I'm new at this, Jay. I don't have much relationship experience but I do know women. And I know *you*."

"Yeah. You do."

"Listen, before Asher kicks us out so he can have his way with Meeka, I need to talk to him."

"Have his way …? They're a thing now?" Jay looked behind her over her shoulder. "Huh."

"You haven't noticed the way he looks at her?"

"Oh, I've noticed," Jay turned back to me. "I just didn't realize that you have as well."

"Practice, baby." I kissed her hard on the mouth. "All fucking practice."

"Whatever you say." She patted my arm.

Sass. So much fucking sass.

I whistled, silencing the room. "I know we haven't met up in a while. We're going to change that." I looked down at Jay. "Right?"

She rolled her eyes but nodded.

Not caring in the least who was watching, I cupped her nape in a rough hold. "The next time you roll your eyes at me, I won't care who is watching. I'll bend you over my lap, rip down those sexy as sin leather pants, and slap that beautiful ass of yours until you're begging me to fuck you."

A flush of pink caressed her cheeks.

And *that* was exactly where I wanted her.

***

(Jay)

After we left Asher's, I couldn't stop thinking about the chat I had with Meeka.

"I'm still pissed at you. I probably will be for a while. But I have a boyfriend who loves me and wants me to be happy and not having my sisters at my back makes me very upset." I raised my hand, stopping Meeka from interrupting me. *"I love you. I love all of you. You're my life, and now Angel is a part of this life as well. You have told me over and over why you did what you did, but I still don't forgive you. You used me. Even though you brought my sister home to me, you still used me as fucking bait."*

Meeka nodded, her eyes shining with unshed tears.

"Have we ever been close, Meeka?" I asked her, staring straight ahead.

"No," she replied, automatically. *"Why am I in the King's Harlots?"*

"Because you're best friends with Brogan."

"That shouldn't matter. That shouldn't ..."

"What?" I turned to her. *"What do you want me to say? That we can be all fine and dandy, go shopping and do each other's hair after what you did?"*

"I never meant for it to go down that way," she pleaded with me. *"Please believe me."*

"God, I feel like such a bitch," I said later that evening, pacing back and forth.

"You're not one, though. You try to be but it's not you." Angel leaned against the headboard, crossing his arms under his chest.

"And who made you Mr. Know It All?"

He raised an eyebrow, challenging me.

I huffed, opening my dresser drawer. Grabbing a pair of pajamas, I slammed the door closed. "I can't deal with her right now. I love her, yes. Of course I do. But right now, I can't stand to be in the same room as her."

GRIM

"That will change," was all Angel said.

But it wasn't what I wanted to hear. I wanted him to tell me that everything would be okay, that it was normal for me to feel this way. Even her voice grated on my nerves. Maybe I had been too harsh. Maybe I should have understood. What if I was in the same situation? Would I have done the same thing as her? I didn't know. I *couldn't* know. Meeka was an only child. She didn't understand the sibling bond. Violet and I were twins. Twins! Our bond was stronger than anyone. But as each day passed, that bond slipped away into nothing. While Violet remained holed up in her house, I spent my time with Angel. He was all I wanted at the moment.

CHAPTER FIVE

Angel

I CRAVED HER screams. My name leaving Jay's lips left me open and undone. Skin slapping against skin. Bodies moving as one. Slick and spent. Exhausted and aching. Jay was who I lived for. And fucking her was just an added bonus.

Her body was made for me. She handled my cock like we had always been connected. I couldn't get enough of her, and I didn't want to.

I loved this woman. So damn much. I would make her my wife, and I would spend the rest of my days showing her just how much she meant to me.

"Scream for me. Louder. Harder. Open your sweet body to me. Show me how much you want me. You like my marks on your pale body."

Words left my mouth of their own accord. Dark. Possessive. Dangerous. And all she did was moan in response.

Jay liked it when I took what I needed from her, knowing she would get what she craved in return.

We worked well together. We were made for each other.

"Angel, please," she panted. "Fuck me harder."

"I'm going to fuck you so hard you'll forget your name." Sinking my teeth into her shoulder, I held her against me.

She whimpered, shaking beneath me and unable to move. She couldn't leave. She was right where I wanted her to be. And I would never let her go.

An hour later and I was standing in front of the punching bag in my basement. But everything hurt. My dick felt like it was going to fall off but giving Jay the pleasure she craved was well worth it in the end.

For whatever reason, I couldn't get enough of her. As each day passed, the sex became more and longer. Not that either of us were complaining but even I knew that we needed to talk. We masked it by fucking hard and often.

I sighed, landing my fist against the heavy bag in front of me.

Everything was turning to shit in a hand basket. I had no idea what the fuck was going on, and it was starting to piss me off.

"Angel?"

A hot shiver raced down my back at the smooth feminine voice coming from behind me. My dick jumped. Adjusting myself, I turned slowly.

Jay caught the movement, her gaze zeroing in on my crotch. "Um …" She coughed, clearing her throat. "The phone is for you."

I smirked, closing the distance between us, and took the phone from her hand before capturing her mouth in a hard kiss.

She sighed, leaning into me.

Placing another soft peck on her lips, I grumbled at whoever was on the phone. It had better be damn important. "Yeah."

"Well, don't we sound fucking cheery?"

I frowned. "Who is this?"

"Your worst nightmare." The deep voice laughed. "How's that for a cliché?"

"If you don't tell me who this is, I'll trace your call and find you." I did not have the patience for this shit.

"So damn touchy, Angel." The man tsked. "You've never had any patience, have you?"

"Who the hell is this and how the fuck do you know my name?"

"How about you use that damn brain? Who do you think it is?"

The voice sounded familiar. But it couldn't be. "Charles Brian."

"Ding ding ding." Charles laughed.

Fuck my life.

***

(Jay)

Angel paced back and forth, rubbing the back of his neck and cursing at Charles. He was still on the phone giving Angel a hard time

I was lucky in the fact that I had never met Charles. Everything in me told me that he was worse than Vega. I had tried so hard to forget. I knew that every time Angel looked at me, he was concerned that I would snap or fall apart until I was a crumbling heaping mess. But I was strong. My daddy raised me well. My chest panged. I made a mental note to call him. Things had been strained with Tyler showing his face around more and more. I attempted to convince my father to kick him out of his club but to no avail. Fucking fucker liked to dig his claws into everything and everyone I held dearly.

"Listen," Angel shouted, "you bastards already shit on my doorstep once. I won't let you get to me a second time." Angel's gaze darkened. "I will enjoy pissing on your grave." He hung up, took a deep breath, and turned my way.

We stood there. Staring at each other. Not knowing what the other was thinking but I could see the evil in his gaze. The pure hatred for the men who were ruining the lives of our small town. The sick sadistic freaks who would do anything to get the control they craved, not caring in the least who they hurt or killed in the process.

"Jay," Angel said gently.

"I get it," I told him.

He closed the distance between us and wrapped his arms around me. "I know you're strong and you can take care of yourself, but I need you to try and let me protect you."

Leaning back, I stared up at him. "Why wouldn't I?"

"Because you're headstrong and determined to make a mark in this world. By yourself," he reminded me.

Oh, yeah. "I'm not stupid, Angel. I know when I need help and this shit is different. After … after Vega …" I swallowed hard. "I can't go through that again."

"I know, baby." He cradled my head against his chest. "I'm sorry. That's not what I meant. You're the strongest woman I know but I need to protect you. I have to. If something …" His voice trailed off.

I agreed with him. I couldn't lose him. We couldn't lose each other. Angel never knew how to love until he met me. And I didn't know what true love was until I met *him*. What I had with Tyler was not love. It was dark and dangerous. Angel wouldn't hurt me—I knew that—but Tyler fucked me up and that tiny sense of dread would probably always be there.

We held each other for what felt like hours, taking the comfort that we needed. No words were said. No noise was made. It was peaceful except for the racing of my heart. I loved this man in my arms. More than my next breath. He was all I needed to survive this shit called life. He made me feel strong. All of this time, I thought I was helping him when really, he had helped me. More than I could ever thank him for. More than I could even say.

"You should call Meeka," Angel said awhile later.

"Why?" I knew why but I didn't want to admit it. She hurt me. We had always butted heads, but I still loved her like a sister. I knew that but I couldn't get over what her and Asher did. Not yet. Maybe not ever.

"I know you're pissed." Angel pulled back, cupping my chin. "Hell, so am I. But you need all the support you can get. You're trying to make a name for your club the legal way. You need all of your sisters at your back."

"Why do you always have to be right?" I grumbled.

He chuckled. "Because I know what's best for you and I also know that you'll feel better once you talk to her."

"What if she hurts me again?" I muttered. I wasn't one to get scared over the small shit but Meeka keeping my sister's safety from me really ate at me. And the fact I was used as bait. Not like it was a big deal or anything. I bit back a scoff.

"You can't think like that. You'll drive yourself fucking crazy." He turned me in his arms and kissed the side of my neck. "Go call her," he said, patting me gently on the rear.

I huffed but did as I was told.

"Hello?" came a soft voice on the other end of the phone.

"Hey," I greeted, sitting on the couch in the living room.

"Jay? Is something wrong?" Meeka asked.

"No. I will be honest, though. Angel is the one who convinced me to call you." I cleared my throat. "I'm trying here, Meeka, but with you not around, it makes it hard."

"I know." She sighed. "We're stopping by tonight." She continued when I didn't say anything, "I miss you girls. This … shit … sucks."

I laughed. She was right.

"I'm happy Angel convinced you to call me."

"Yeah, well, that man of mine is too fucking smart for his own good sometimes." I cleared my throat again. "Max wanted to have a party tonight, but I told her to just have the guys and us there."

"I agree. I need to see you girls."

"How are things there?"

Meeka laughed. "I have a dark, brooding man who won't leave me alone and it's confusing as hell."

"Sounds like you got a problem," I teased.

"A delicious one," she whispered.

"Listen, whatever you do, whatever is going on between the both of you, don't be stupid like I was and push him away."

"Why, Jay, are you giving me advice?" Meeka teased back.

This light hearted humor was a nice change. "Yeah, I guess I am."

"Baby, who are you talking to?" Angel asked, a slight smirk spreading on his face.

"Meeka," I replied.

"God, woman, it's about damn time," Angel grumbled.

I rolled my eyes.

"I'll let you go, Jay," Meeka said. "Thank you again for calling me."

"See you tonight." And with that, I hung up.

"How did it go?" Angel sat beside me on the couch, grabbing hold of my hand. He slipped his fingers between mine, brushing his thumb back and forth over mine.

"Good." I leaned my head against his shoulder. "Thank you."

"If you haven't realized it by now, I would do anything to make you happy." He kissed my nose. "Remember that."

GRIM

(Angel)

"Oh, God. Yes. Angel. More. Please."

Jay's begging was music to my fucking ears. Her hips bucked against my face. Her pussy soaked and glistening. She tasted like heaven and I was a starved man, devouring my meal.

Once we arrived at the clubhouse, no one had been around. I threw her over my shoulder and charged for her room before she could protest and fight against me.

I growled like an animal and lapped at her center. Thrusting my tongue in and out of her, I flicked her swollen clit with my finger until she came a third time.

She moaned.

Wrapping my arms around her hips, I pulled her against me and ate at her hard and rough. She would have razor burn and slight bruising, but the caveman inside of me didn't fucking care.

My senses were on overdrive as her sweetness slid down my throat. I didn't let up. It only made me suck and lick harder.

This unexpected urge to make her break took over. It consumed my soul. All of the stress, not knowing what was going on, our own personal issues ... it all drove me to the brink of madness. Everything I felt, I took it out on Jay. My fiancée. My Queen. The piece of me I never knew I needed.

After Jay came undone a fourth time, I flipped her onto her stomach and drove my body into hers so hard, we both shouted out. Not caring in the least who heard us, I forced the screams to leave her mouth. The cries of pleasure to grace my ears. The hard demands for me to be rougher.

God, I loved this woman and everything she was. I lived and breathed her. My feelings for her grew strong and fast in the short time we had been together. I thanked God for her every day and I would spend the rest of my life proving to her that she deserved better than what Tyler had given her.

"I love you, my Queen," I whispered in her ear an hour later. Kissing her shoulder, I cupped her breast in my hand and threw my leg over hers.

"I love you." She sighed, curling into me. "Max is throwing a party just for Vice-One and us. It'll be good for everyone to unwind."

"Fucking you eases my stress but if she wants a party, I won't be rude."

Jay laughed. "Thank you." Sitting up, she let the sheet fall to her waist. The metal barbells poking through her nipples sparkled in the late afternoon sun.

"You are so fucking beautiful," I groaned, my dick twitching.

Her cheeks flushed. "Yeah? Just how beautiful am I?" She licked her lips and straddled my lap.

"You're so beautiful, it takes my breath." I gripped her hips, pushing into her before she had a chance to stop me.

She moaned, throwing her head back.

My cock slid into her center. She was wet, needy, so fucking hungry for me. "Ride me, Jay."

Her hips circled against mine, slamming hard into my pelvis.

I groaned, meeting her thrust for thrust. "That's it," I reared up. "Take what you need from me. Fuck me hard."

Her hands slapped against my chest, digging her nails into my pecs. "God, you feel good."

"So do you." I flipped her onto her back, thrusting into her hard before crashing my mouth to hers. It wasn't just a kiss. It was the need to consume. The ultimate battle between who owned who. We enjoyed the back and forth, the cat and mouse play, but in the end, we both owned each other.

CHAPTER SIX

Jay

MAX THREW A party. Of course she would. It was the only way she could get out of her head. Whenever there was a problem, she would put together a gathering. She needed to socialize for fear of losing herself.

After all of the shit she had to endure with Dale Michaels, she did everything in her power to forget.

I had been a shitty friend and wasn't there for her when she needed me most. Although she had reassured me that everything was fine between us, I could sense the hint of jealousy seeping from her pores. It took everything in me not to beat Dale's face in. The fucker got her pregnant but wanted nothing to do with her or the baby.

"What's wrong, princess?" Angel asked, kissing my forehead.

"Ev … nothing."

He frowned but didn't argue with me.

Had it come to this? Did he now take my lies for what they were? Even though he knew I had been lying, he never questioned me.

After being together for months, I still couldn't get over the fact that he had taken control of me where I needed it most. I did everything I could to give it to him willingly. He never took me for granted. But the part I had lost so long ago with Tyler still forced its way into my mind.

"I love you."

He didn't.

"You are everything to me."

That wasn't true.

"You're mine."

Which meant he could fuck anyone he wanted to but if I so much as looked at another man, Tyler's fist would end up against my face. Or worse. It was always worse.

The first time he hit me, it shocked me to the core. I had been so surprised, I thought it wasn't real. But being raised by my father and his bike club, I hit Tyler back without even thinking. Of course, he enjoyed it and it turned into the darkest dirtiest sex I ever had.

Every emotion, every hint of the love I thought I had felt for my ex was replaced from the first moment Angel looked at me. We enjoyed challenging each other. The violence I had endured with Tyler came so often I found myself getting used to it.

"Jay?"

I rose from the bed and turned toward Angel. Standing there naked, completely stripped bare for the man I loved, I waited.

"I love you," he finally said.

"I love you too," I whispered back. And I did. More than life. He was my sun, moon, and stars. The beginning to my end. My everything. But I didn't know how to give him all of me in return. I knew I had to. I prayed. Begged for the words to leave my mouth to let him know that I was fucked up. To help him realize that I was just scared. The words never left my lips.

Under normal circumstances, Angel would have demanded that I join him in bed. He would then make promises to fill my mind and my body with only him. But I wasn't in the mood. Not for him. Not for anyone. It wasn't fair to him. None of this was his fault. It was the whole "it's not you, it's me" bullshit and it pissed me off even more.

Angel slid his legs over the side of the bed, brushing a hand through his dark hair. "I love you," he repeated. "Know that. And I will spend the rest of my life showing you that I'm not him."

My heart jumped. "I don't know what you're talking about."

Angel let out a heavy sigh. "You don't have to admit it. Not yet. I'll give you time, Jay, but I mean it. I am not Tyler. I can be an asshole. I know that. But I would never do anything to you that you didn't want me to do. Please know that I love you."

"I do." I got dressed and headed for the door, needing to run away from his words. There was no way I could discuss Tyler at the moment. "I'm going to get a bottle of the strongest alcohol I have."

Angel grunted, pulling on his jeans and t-shirt. "Sounds like a perfect plan."

"Or a dangerous one," I mumbled.

We left my room and walked hand in hand down the hall. We were having issues talking but that small touch gave me some hope. It wasn't a lot, but it was a start.

Before we reached the crowded area at the front of the club, Angel stopped me and kissed my knuckles. He stared intently into my eyes, backing me up against the wall.

A breath left me on a whoosh. I would never get used to seeing this side of him. The dark and dominating man who took from me what he needed and gave me what I craved in return.

Brushing the back of his knuckles down the side of my face, he placed his other hand on the wall.

I was caged in by this man. I knew everything about him. What to expect. But I would never get used to how, with one look, he took my breath away.

His dark eyes burned me, searing into my skin until all I could focus on was him staring back at me.

"You are so damn beautiful," he gritted, his jaw clenching. "Your beauty makes me weak."

"Angel," I breathed, sliding my hands down his chest and leaning my forehead against him.

"I love you, Jay. Nothing will change that," he gripped the back of my neck in a firm hold, reminding me that I belonged to him. And I did, didn't I? Every inch of me. Every single fiber of my very being.

But what if something *did* change things? What if Tyler succeeded in ruining our relationship? He didn't want me, but he didn't want anyone else to have me, either. I knew how he worked. He would get in our heads, trying to take control from the inside out.

"Jay, stop fucking thinking so much," Angel pinched my chin, forcing me to look up at him. "I know you worry. I do too. We can't see the future. I have no idea what tomorrow will bring. But I do know that I will always fucking love you. I just wish you would believe me."

Tears welled in my eyes, my throat constricting. It was so damn tight, every swallow I made burned like hell. "I know," I whispered.

"Do you?" he demanded, releasing me. He took a step back, shoving his hand through his hair. "My life is shit without you, but I won't beg you to stay. If you want out, show me the respect I deserve and tell me."

My eyes widened. "What? God no." I closed the distance between us, gripping his thick arms. "Of course I don't want out. You have to believe me. I love you. I love you with all of me." I rambled on and on but Angel wouldn't meet my gaze. He didn't believe me. Was this because of Tyler? Or me? *Shit. What have I done?*

Nothing. That's what. I have done nothing at all to show Angel how much I loved him. Both of us had difficulty with words but I never thought it would end us.

"Let's make an appearance at Max's party," Angel muttered, his deep voice soon drowned out by the loud music.

I followed him out into the crowded room.

Angel and his brothers had fixed up the hole in the far wall. Looking at it, you would never think that months ago, someone attempted to blow the place up.

And that was when I met him. For the first time.

GRIM

Angel Rodriguez.
My King.

CHAPTER SEVEN

Angel

JAY'S LAUGHTER VIBRATED into my soul. It was melodious, sliding over my skin like melted chocolate. But it was an act. Every single smile, every giggle, none of it was real. Because of me. Anyone who knew her would see that the smiles never reached her eyes. Or that the laughter was forced and drawn out.

She would look my way every so often, her eyes pleading with me to stay. But it wasn't me she had to worry about.

Jay would run. I knew it. *She* knew it. I was just waiting for the time to come when I would wake up in the morning to an empty spot in bed beside me.

"I need a fucking drink."

Jay's loud demand sent my nerves on edge.

I didn't know these men, these bikers. Her father's club hadn't even made an appearance. At least with them, I knew what to expect. Dickface Tyler, on the other hand, was another thing.

"Grab a bottle and bring it back to your room," I called out over the music, leaning against the wall.

"Not gonna happen, baby," she yelled back. "I'm getting drunk with my sisters tonight. You can join me if you wish." Her gaze challenged me. With her chin jutted out, her lips pursed into a straight line. She wanted to fight.

But unfortunately for her, I was not in the mood. Playing along, I heaved out a heavy sigh. "Fine. If I must."

She laughed. Standing on tiptoes, she gave me a soft kiss on the mouth. "Come." She grabbed my hand, leading me to one of the larger booths at the front of the room.

"Jay." I wrapped my arm around her waist, pulling her close. "We need to talk."

"Not right now," she insisted. "Please. I love you. And I know you love me. Let's just have that for right now."

I wasn't the type of guy who could just close off my feelings and mask it with a shell of happy. It didn't work that way.

But happy wife. Happy life.

She wasn't my wife yet, but she damn well would be. And soon.

"We're talking later." I kissed her hard on the mouth. "And you are not getting shit faced tonight."

"Why the hell not?"

"Because I need my girlfriend tonight." I pinched her chin, forcing her to look me in the eye. "I need my *fiancée*."

Jay didn't say anything, but she didn't argue with me, either.

Sliding into the booth, she reached out for my hand.

I sat beside her, wrapping an arm around her shoulders.

She joked and laughed, chatting with people around her. But I knew her inside and out. She was rigid, rubbing her temples every so often as if warding off an impending headache.

Despite our love being hard and fast, I could see it. It had been the same thing over and over for the past couple of weeks. Even when we first started dating. The twinge of anxiety in my gut hinted at the fact she wasn't revealing all to me. She was scared, terrified that I would leave her or worse. Tyler had fucked up her sense of worth. Her trust in men. That a man wouldn't hurt her. That is what he did to her. And that is what I was trying to change.

Jay talked.

I listened.

The party had taken off, people milling in and out of the clubhouse. Max had set up the gathering but she was nowhere in sight. While she and Dale had their problems, he refused to talk about it. Flirting and drinking with women who took his mind off the fact he got Max pregnant. The fucker wasn't happy. Not with the situation or even how he was dealing with things, but he masked it by ignoring it.

And I thought *I* had issues coming to terms with how I felt.

As if her ears had been burning, Max appeared from the hallway leading into the back of the club. She caught my gaze, gave a small wave, and started walking toward us.

My back stiffened, knowing she would see Dale with the two women who were all over him.

"Jay." I tugged my girlfriend's hand gently. "Max."

Jay followed the direction of my gaze. "Shit."

Before she could say anything, I slid out of the booth, giving her the room to make her way toward her best friend. Max wasn't stupid, but she didn't need to see Dale's shit, either.

"How about we go take a walk?" Jay stepped in front of Max, shielding her view, but she wasn't quick enough.

Max peered around her, saw Dale, and paused. Shaking her head, she turned around and walked away.

I was surprised. Expecting her to lose her shit, I never took her for calm and collected. Maybe she had enough. Maybe Dale took it too far.

"Dale," I called out, interrupting his moment with the whores in his lap.

"What?" He frowned, pushing one of the women off of him. He adjusted himself before standing to his full height.

Fucker. "Don't be a dick."

Raising an eyebrow, he crossed his arms over his chest. "Since when do you care what I do?"

"What the hell is that supposed to mean?" I closed the distance between us, getting in his face. "You hurt my fiancée's best friend? You hurt my fiancée. You don't want to do that."

"What are you going to do about it, Angel? You going to hit me? You going to force Max to talk to me and sort this shit out? No? Didn't think so." He sidestepped around me, stomping his way to the door. "Until she decides to talk to me, I'll do whatever the *fuck* I want."

"Have you tried talking to *her*?" I yelled back, following him. "She told you she loved you and look at how you reacted."

"You're hanging out with these women too much," he mumbled, slumping onto the picnic table. "You're getting soft."

"Well, excuse me for caring."

"You care?" Dale scoffed. "You're fucking funny."

"What the hell is this about? I told you I was sorry. I told you I never knew how to tell you, my brothers, that you have helped me through so much and that I love you. But I've finally said it, haven't I? Shouldn't that be enough?"

Dale raised an eyebrow. "Seriously? You're asking me that? Why don't you try showing us how you feel instead of saying it? Maybe then you can get through to your fiancée as well and she won't look at you like she wants to gut you."

"I ..." My mouth opened and closed. He was right. God, I was so stupid.

"Funny, isn't it? You're engaged and the guy who fucked everything up with his woman sets you straight."

I sat beside him, dropping my head in my hands. "I ... fuck."

"Yup. Exactly." Dale shook his head.

"What about you and Max?"

"There is no me and Max."

"Have you tried?" As soon as the question left my lips, a dark shadow appeared out of the corner of my eye. It moved fast but not fast enough before I caught who it was.

"Fucking Tyler." Dale took the word right out of my mouth.

"What the hell do you want?" I barked, jumping off the table.

"I came to talk to Jenny," Tyler stated, making his way to the front of the club. The fact that he called her by that name irritated the fuck out of me. It was a name only he had given her. Call it jealousy, but every time he used it, I wanted to drive my fist into his face.

"I don't fucking think so." I stepped in his way, blocking him.

"You going to stop me? If I want to talk to her, I will, whether either of you like it or not." Tyler stepped around me.

Reaching a hand out, I grabbed hold of his leather cut and pushed him back. "Not happening. Jay is busy."

"No, I'm not." Jay came up beside me, crossing her arms over her chest. I really wished she wouldn't have done that. The small move pushed up her tits, making them look fuller.

Tyler's gaze followed the movement, his tongue peeking out to lick along his bottom lip.

An inhuman growl left my mouth, and before I could comprehend what I was doing, I jumped him.

Yelling and screaming sounded around me, but all I could focus on was the piece of shit beneath me. My fist flew into his face.

He laughed, attempting to push me back.

Heavy arms wrapped around my shoulders, pulling me, but I wouldn't budge. This asshole needed to be taught a lesson. He needed to know that Jay was no longer his. She was mine. She would marry me. She would spend the rest of her life with me. And any children Jay would have will be mine and hers. Tyler could go fuck himself. And stay the fuck away from my woman.

***

(Jay)

"I'm leaving you," I told Tyler, packing the little clothing I had, in my bag.

Tyler didn't say anything as he lit a smoke and inhaled. Blowing out the cloud of toxins, he only watched me.

I had always thought he was beautiful in a hard domineering kind of way. He was the bad boy. And I was the good girl. He wanted to break me, and when he did, he got bored. But after all of the shit we had been through, I would always be grateful to him. He taught me to be strong, but he also taught me that there is no such thing as true love.

"Are you going to say anything?" I asked, sitting on the edge of his bed. The sheets were crumpled, memories of what we had done only a half an hour before sliding into my mind.

"Why should I?" he finally said, taking another long drag of his cigarette.

"You're not surprised."

"Nope." Tyler leaned forward, stretching his thick arms up over his head. The muscles moved and rippled over his hard body, the tattoos that adorned his skin moving as if they were alive.

I loved him. In a sick and very twisted way, I would always love him.

"Do you love me? Honestly. After everything we have been through, do you love me?" I needed to know. He had been there for me when my sister disappeared. He was the only one who believed me that she didn't just run off with some random person.

"I love you," he repeated the words but the emotion never reached his eyes. "But I also got what I wanted and now that I have it——" he shrugged "—I don't need you anymore."

My heart jumped. Expecting tears to fall, I was shocked with myself when I didn't feel any remorse. I was done. Finished. Everything I'd had with Tyler Bone was over.

"As much as I hate you, thank you for being there for me with my … my sister."

Tyler rose to his feet and came toward me. The scent of sex wafted into my nose. "Jenny," he growled, pinching my chin. "Say it again."

"What?"

"Say it," he demanded, forcing my head back.

"I hate you."

He smirked. "Good."

Watching my boyfriend kick my ex's ass was not something I expected to see anytime soon. Tyler egged Angel on. Pushing and poking until he snapped. I should have done something about it. I should have stopped them. But Tyler deserved it. He had it coming. Year after year of fighting with him surfaced to the forefront of my mind. Memories of pain. That moment of disgust for hitting him back. I always knew that Tyler deserved it, but two wrongs never made a right. My conscience told me that it was not okay. Violence didn't solve anything. I knew that even though I never listened.

While Angel punched Tyler, I only stood there. Everything in me told me to stop him. But I couldn't. My feet were stuck, my body immobile. It was like I was having an out-of-body experience as I looked down at the huddle on the ground. Words flew around me.

Tyler pushed Angel off of him, finally breaking free of him. "You fucking pussy. You think fighting me solves anything? I live for this shit. Just ask your girlfriend."

"You bastard," Angel growled, clenching his bloody hands at his sides. "You think I don't know what you did to her? You think I don't know the scars you left on her fucking soul?"

My chest constricted at Angel's badgering of questions. We never talked about what I went through with Tyler. Maybe we should have. I told Angel that he was a monster and our relationship had been toxic but nothing more came of that. The rumors flew around, people talked. Tyler had been abusive, but I was just as bad.

"Angel," I finally said.

"Everything I did was because she asked for it," Tyler shot back, shoving Angel. "I'm an asshole, but I'm not abusive."

I scoffed. "No?" I took a step forward. "You think the bruises I had were because I fell?"

"Jay." Angel cupped my shoulder, squeezing gently.

"You think I asked for you to hit me?" I shrugged Angel off, not needing his pity at the moment. "You think because we got in arguments, that I didn't listen, whatever the reason was, that it gave you the right to smack me around?"

"You hit me back." Tyler narrowed his eyes. "Does Angel hit you?"

"The fact that you're even asking that is fucking hilarious." I pasted a smile on my face. "Angel would never hit me. That makes him more of a man than you will ever be." I turned to walk away when Tyler's next words stopped me.

"Did you tell him that you met me for lunch?"

GRIM

A bone-chilling dread washed over me as I watched the emotions change in Angel's eyes before me. It went from sympathy to anger in a split second. Never in my life would I think that anger would be directed at me. But making the stupid mistake of meeting up with Tyler came back to bite me in the ass.

"I only met with you to tell you to leave me alone," I told him, keeping my eyes on Angel. "I also remember telling you that I'm happy." I needed Angel to know that I didn't meet with Tyler because I wanted to. Angel was everything to me. He was the best thing for me. I knew that it was time for us to talk. For everything to come out. I would give him the dark, violent details of what I went through with Tyler. I would give Angel … everything.

"Is that so? How come you stayed with me for an hour then?"

My back stiffened.

Angel looked over my head, and when his gaze landed back on mine, I swore my life had officially ended. I would rather deal with the shit with Vega again then see Angel look at me like I had just ripped out his soul.

"Angel, he's trying to piss you off." I closed the distance between us, placing my hands on his strong chest. "It was innocent. I wasn't keeping track of the time. Please believe me."

Angel's hands clenched into fists at his sides. "Why should I?"

"Because I love you. Only you. I was meeting him to put an end to this shit. Please believe me." We had been together for months, but I never thought it would come to this.

Tyler laughed. "See, Jenny? You should just drop this bastard and come back to where you belong."

"Shut up," I screamed, turning on him. "You!" I charged for him, shoving him back. "You've put this wrench in my relationship. You can't be happy for me. You're a sick controlling fuck who gets his rocks off on destroying people's lives. My dad should have fucking killed you by now."

"Fuck you, you little whore," Tyler spat, shoving me back. "I'm not done with you. I've never been done with you."

"Watch who you're talking to." Angel pulled me behind him. "I don't know what the hell you think is going on between you two, but she belongs to me. Me! She's *my* fucking woman. I am going to marry her and give her the life that *you* couldn't."

"It's funny …" Tyler peered around Angel. "You've never needed a man to fight your battles before. Why now?"

I looked away, my cheeks heating. I didn't need Angel to fight for me. He knew that. But sometimes a girl needed the strength of a man to protect her. *Safe.* I was comfortable with him and could act like myself. I didn't have to worry about him blowing up and hitting me for no reason at all. But why was I so damn scared that it would happen? Angel wasn't Tyler. He wasn't. I realized that now. It felt like a ton of bricks had finally been lifted. Meeting with Tyler would cause a fight, I knew that when I agreed to see him, but the fight would be worth it in the end if I got the closure I finally needed.

"Well, this has been fun as always—" Tyler chuckled "—but I'm going to join the party that I wasn't invited to."

"Like hell you are." Angel pushed him back. "I beat your ass once, I'll do it again."

"Why didn't you invite me to the party, Jenny?" Tyler asked, ignoring his threat.

A mumbled voice came from behind me.

"Did you have something to say?" Tyler glared past me.

Asher took a step forward.

I realized then that Angel and I were no longer alone. The Harlots and Vice-One were standing around us, ready to take on our battle.

"Not yet." Meeka moved in front of Asher, placing a hand on his chest. "Don't."

Tyler chuckled. "You men call yourselves Navy SEALs? I wouldn't want you protecting my country. You're worthless as shit and you let women tell you what to do."

"We don't let anyone tell us what to do, but we're also not stupid enough to go against them." Angel stepped up beside me, placing his hand on the small of my back.

I stood taller, jutting out my chin. "You're not welcome here, Tyler." Even though I had told him that over and over again, with Angel's touch on my back, I was able to pull the strength from him. We had shit to deal with but we were still one.

"You see, the funny thing is that I'm always welcome. You don't have a choice because your dad still owns this property." Tyler smirked. "I'm right, aren't I?"

"What's he talking about, Jay?" Max asked, placing her hands on her hips. The movement caused her tiny bump to become more pronounced.

"He's not talking about anything," I bit out. "You're full of shit, Tyler. My dad has nothing to do with this place. I am the one who bought it. I am the one who pays to keep this fucking place maintained. You can tell my father *that*."

"Oh, he already knows." Tyler leaned forward, brushing a strand of hair behind my ear. "Do you think of me when he fucks you?"

A deep growl came from Angel. "You motherfucker." He charged for Tyler, pushing him back a foot. "I'll kill you. This time I will fucking beat you."

"Try it, asshole." But Tyler only laughed. He actually laughed at Angel.

In a quick move, Asher had his arms around Angel's shoulders, pulling him back.

"You need to leave," I said, my voice unexpectedly calm. "Right now. Before I tell Asher to let Angel go."

Tyler threw his head back and laughed again. "God, you haven't changed."

"I've had enough," Meeka interrupted. "You come in here, expecting a grand entrance, and when you don't get the reaction you want, you get pissy. Or maybe you *did* get the reaction you wanted. Were you trying to get a rise out of Jay? Does it turn you on knowing her boyfriend is ready to kick your ass? *I* should just tell Asher to let him go."

"Who do you think you are, little girl?" Tyler snapped at her.

"She's my fucking sister, so you leave her the hell alone." I got in his face. Even though he was a head taller than me, there was no way I was backing down.

"Oh, yeah, Jenny." Tyler licked his lips. "I remember how our fights went. Maybe we should give your boyfriend a little show."

And that was when he kissed me. All thoughts shut off as my mind took me back to years before. Tyler's kisses had been demanding, forcing me to into a submission I didn't want. He scared me, utterly terrified me that I had now been permanently broken because of him.

"You liked that," Tyler whispered, his eyes darkening.

I did. Only because I knew finally, that it was officially over between us.

A small smile tugged at my lips.

Tyler frowned, knowing full well there would never be another chance with me. He became possessive in the end, and luckily, I was able to get out.

Suddenly, I was pulled away from him.

Angel's fists flew into Tyler's jaw. Before it was rough but now, it turned violent. He pummeled him to the ground, hitting and beating Tyler like he was the punching bag in our gym.

My feet remained glued to the ground. I stood there. Doing nothing. Not attempting in the least to pull these two men apart. Men who had come into my life at different times and took what they needed from me. Tyler grasped my soul, squeezing it until I was a shattered mess. But Angel took that mess and cleaned it up, putting all of my broken pieces back together again.

I had heard of a darkness living inside of us. Coby, who I hardly spoke to, had it. I could see it in his eyes.

"Should we stop him?" someone asked.

"Not yet." That was Coby.

For whatever reason, I trusted him the most besides Angel.

I closed my eyes, took a deep breath, and nodded once.

"Now," Coby demanded, his voice gruff.

Asher and Stone pulled Angel off of Tyler.

He didn't fight them, but when he walked past me, I kept my gaze on Tyler.

Angel leaned down to my ear. "You *will* explain why you liked it when he kissed you."

My breath caught.

Dale and Stone picked Tyler up off the ground. He only smirked, rubbing his jaw. A dark bruise had already started to set in. Blood was dripping from his nose. Fucker was grinning like a Cheshire cat.

I didn't say anything as Dale and Stone pushed him forward.

"You need to leave," Dale barked. "*Now.*"

"What's going on with you two, Jay?" Max asked, grabbing my hand.

"He's an asshole," I mumbled.

"No, I mean with you and Angel."

"Yeah." My eyes welled. "I know." And with that, I walked away.

Voices followed me into the clubhouse, but I couldn't make out who was saying what. I didn't care. I could only focus on the fact that Angel almost killed Tyler. A thought crossed my mind, forcing bile to rise in my throat.

It would make things a hell of a lot easier if Tyler was dead.

Had it officially come to this? Was I desperate to hold onto the love Angel and I shared, that I was considering murdering my ex?

My feet moved of their own accord, taking me to Angel who stood at the bar with Asher and Stone still holding him.

I pushed him.

He only glared down at me, shrugging off his brothers who hadn't let him go.

"What the hell was that?" I demanded, pushing him again. "You can't do that, Angel. I don't need men after you because you're fucking jealous."

"I am not jealous." He frowned. "You are mine, and no man, I don't care who the fuck he is, gets to lay his mouth on you."

"That doesn't mean you should beat him within an inch of his life," I shouted, smacking him in the chest. "You have no idea who he is or what he's capable of."

"Please." Angel rolled his eyes. "He's still alive, isn't he? I've been to fucking war. You think I'm scared of some bastard who can't let my girlfriend go?"

"I don't care about that shit." I grabbed his shirt, pulling him close. "I care about you. That's it. It would kill me if something happened to you."

"Nothing will happen to me as long as he stays the hell away from you."

We stood there in silence, staring at each other.

My blood pounded in my ears. The scent of sweat wafted into my nose, making it tingle. "What if he doesn't?" I asked, crossing my arms over my chest. "I can't control what they do, and you can't jump him every time he comes by."

"Then he needs to stay away."

I agreed with him, but there was no way I could make that happen. "He's the vice-president of my dad's club. That's not going to happen."

"Make it happen."

"Angel," I bit out. "You know I can't do that."

"Are you sure?" Angel raised an eyebrow. "Or is it because you don't want to?"

My mouth opened and closed. "Are you seriously asking me this?"

"I am. Tell me, princess. Why did you like it when he kissed you?"

I moved past him. "I'm not talking about this with you in front of everyone. You have an issue with me, be a man and talk to me, but don't accuse me of shit."

"*Fuck.*"

Exactly.

CHAPTER EIGHT

Angel

I KNEW MY jealousy was going to get the best of me some day when it came to Jay and Tyler. But when he kissed her, actually fucking kissed her and she didn't push him away? All bets were off, and I lost it.

When my fists landed against his face, it was unnerving how much I enjoyed it. How good it felt to get out all of the frustration and pent-up anger that had been building up inside of me for the past couple of weeks.

I needed to fight. Go to war. Have the angriest fucking sex ever. I didn't care. But I needed something. I had an itch that needed scratching. Watching Jay walk away from me made me pissed as hell, but it turned me on.

The words that left my mouth were downright mean and uncalled for but seeing Tyler kiss my girlfriend set something off inside of me. Even though it had been him who started it, I could sense that she enjoyed it. I didn't know how. I didn't know why. But I prayed with everything in me to whoever was paying attention that it was for closure and nothing more.

I didn't like losing control. It didn't sit well with me and made me sick to my stomach. Jay had taught me to love and when I saw another man's lips on hers, that darkness inside of me rejoiced that it could finally come out and play.

Jay pushed open the door to her bedroom . It brought me back to the first time so many months ago. She had left Max's gallery, hot and bothered. I followed her. Fucked her. And fell in love.

But now, this had nothing to do with love, did it?

Jay stomped to her dresser, pulled open a drawer, and slammed it shut. She laughed, turning toward me. "I can't believe you accused me … No, wait. Yes, I can."

And here we go. My jaw clenched, but I didn't say anything.

"I don't know how many times I have to tell you that Tyler and I are over. But your jealousy can't see that. It's one thing for him to not believe me because he's a possessive asshole but you?" She shook her head, her eyes shining. "I love you. I'm *in love* with you. I've agreed to marry you." Her face paled.

I frowned. "Jay?"

She shook her head, swallowing excessively before the color came back into her cheeks. "How can we get married if you don't trust me?"

"I do trust you," I muttered, shoving my hands into the pockets of my jeans.

"Do you? Do you really? Tyler kissed me. Did I enjoy it? Yes."

A growl rumbled from the back of my throat.

"Before you get all Alpha male on me, I enjoyed it because I knew it was officially over. I felt nothing, Angel. Nothing at all. You have to believe me."

I did. But I couldn't get the image of his mouth on hers out of my head. "He needs to stay away."

"He has nothing to do with this." She took a step toward me. "You have to believe me. I'm in love with you, Angel. My King. I can't … God, you make me an emotional wreck because I worry every damn day that you'll leave me."

My chest constricted at her confession. "Why would you think that?" I closed the distance between us, cupping her face. "I love you. You've taught me to love, princess. My Queen." My throat tightened. "I love you. I've been in love with you since the first time I heard your voice. Since the first time you called me an asshole. No woman has gotten under my skin like you have. You are the better part of me. The only part I want."

"Why aren't we getting along then?" A lonely tear rolled down her cheek.

I wiped it away with my thumb, kissing her gently on the mouth. "All of this shit with Charles Brian and his fucking band of bastards, Tyler and his possession of you … It's stressing us the fuck out. We shouldn't take it out on each other."

"Then why are we?" she whispered.

I had no idea how to answer that.

Growing up, I had a hard time believing in love and a higher power. Even being in the Navy made it hard to remain positive. How could a God let these things happen? To make us stronger? To help us grow? I didn't know the answers, but I did know that with Jay by my side, I could get through anything. We would bring Charles down. We would succeed in bringing not only him down, but the whole operation. With the help of her sisters and my brothers, we would end this evil entity that had taken over our town. We had become a family. Of course, with Dale and Max not talking, the sexual tension rising between Asher and Meeka, their issues were distracting.

"I'm sorry," I finally said. "I'm sorry for accusing you of wanting Tyler in your life still."

"I'll talk to my dad. He's the president. Maybe he's grown some balls and can put Tyler in his place." She sighed, running a hand through her hair before pulling it up into a messy bun. "I ..."

"What?" She had stepped out of my hold, but I still touched her. My fingers moved of their own accord. Running down her cheek. Over her jawline. Her full mouth. Her throat. I couldn't stop touching her. She was my life. My strength. She was soft where I was rough. Even though an apology had been said, it still wasn't enough. They were only words. I needed to show her that I meant what I said. That I did love her. That I did want to spend the rest of my life with her.

"I ... I think I need to stay away for a little bit."

"What the ever loving fuck?" I snapped, pushing her back and forcing her to look at me.

"Don't." She shoved out of my grip. "Don't you dare put your hands on me like him."

Shit. "Don't fucking compare me to him," I countered.

"What the hell is wrong with us, Angel?" she yelled, pushing me. "We go from fighting to confessing our love to each other, back to fighting again. I can't do this. Not with you. Not with us. I need you, but I don't need your alpha male bullshit."

I shook my head. "My alpha comes out because of him. Tyler. That fucking bastard starts this every single time we see him. He puts these thoughts into our heads like a mind-fuck, and I can't get them out."

"And whose fault is that, Angel?" Jay leaned against her dresser, gripping the edge with her hands until her knuckles turned white. "I can't do this." Her voice wavered. "I'm tired. I'm so damn tired of us fighting."

Sitting on the edge of her bed, I dropped my head in my hands. I didn't know what to do or how to make it better. Tyler succeeded in tearing us apart.

"I love you," I muttered. "But I don't know how to fix this."

"I think we need some time apart," she mumbled. "We fell into this too fast."

"You can't stand there and tell me that this wasn't meant to be. You are the one who convinced me that there is such a thing as love and a happily ever after." I couldn't take her doubting my love for her.

"Well, maybe it isn't worth it."

My head snapped up. Before I could comprehend what I was doing, I was standing in front of her.

Her eyes widened, taking on that shine I had come to know so well. "What are you going to do?" she asked, her voice shaking.

If I was a gentleman, I would leave her alone. I would give her some space like she had asked. But I wasn't. I was the man she loved with a monster inside of me she loved even more.

***

(Jay)

When Angel charged for me, I was expecting him to throw me over his shoulder and demand I stay. I ran. I always ran. Even when we first got together, I ran. I was terrified he would leave me like my mother and sister had. But when Violet came back, when she was saved from the hands of Hell, Angel was right there by my side. So why the fuck couldn't we go back to that point in time?

"What are you going to do, Angel?" I repeated, staring up at him. I noticed for the first time in weeks that he had bags under his eyes, a peppering of grey showed through the smattering of scruff on his strong jaw. Stress had aged him. Me. His job. Tyler. Me. I leaned my head against his chest, breathing in the scent I had begun to crave months before. "Angel—"

Rough hands spun me, shoving me hard against the dresser. I let out an oomph at the unexpected movement.

"Look at us," Angel growled, his fingers twisting in my hair. He pulled my head back, his lower body pushing into mine. "*Look.*"

My gaze followed his, landing on our reflection in the mirror. His eyes were dark, cold. Angry. His large body loomed over mine, grinding into me until all I felt was him. Everywhere. Every single inch. Every curve of his muscles. Every throbbing vein.

"You see us?"

His voice took on a darkness I had never heard from him before. And as much as it shouldn't have, it turned me on.

"Yes," I whispered, my mouth going dry.

"Look into my eyes," he demanded, wrapping his other hand around my throat. "Tell me I don't love you. Tell me you want this to end."

"I ..."

"Tell me."

"No!" I cried, pushing back against him.

Sliding his hand down into the vee of my t-shirt, he pulled it lower. The red lace of my bra peaked out, taunting him.

"Tell me *you* don't love *me*." With both hands, he ripped my shirt in half.

A gasp left me, a flutter of heat warming my lower belly. "I love you."

"Tell me you don't want to spend the rest of your life with me." Angel's hands reached my hips, his fingers digging into the flesh of my ass. "Tell me you hate me."

I shook my head. "No."

"Fucking tell me." With a roughness I craved, he pulled my leather pants down to my ankles. Kicking my legs apart, he reached between us.

My breathing sped up. Sex didn't solve anything. I knew that. But I didn't care. It would make us feel better. We both knew it. It was how we were wired. We fought. We loved. We fucked.

"Tell me you hate me," he snarled in my ear. A zipper sounded, sending a wave of desire racing through me. "Mmmm … my dirty princess wants me to fucking play."

"Yes," I moaned.

"Tell me you love me." Angel hooked a finger in the string of my thong, shoving it to the side. "Tell me."

"I—" A cry left me when he thrust into me so hard, my feet rose from the floor. "Yes! I love you. I love you. God, Angel."

"Tell me," he bellowed, gripping my ripped shirt and holding my lower body with his thick thighs. His powerful thrusts didn't let up. He didn't let me get used to this new dangerous side of him. He didn't let me do anything, and I loved every single moment of it.

I cried out. I screamed. I cursed. But I loved him even more. All of the words that were said and passed between us. All of the pain and heartache . He was my man. My fiancé. The love of my life. We had issues. We had problems. But we were real. Our love … was real.

"Fuck, Jay." His hand inched up to my throat, his other arm wrapping around my middle. "Tell me."

"I love you," I whimpered, holding onto the dresser.

"Tell me you don't love him."

I knew that was coming.

Something had changed in Angel when Tyler kissed me. A dark, possessive man took over. I had never seen it before in him but I understood. If I saw a woman kissing Angel, I would have reacted the same way.

"I don't love him," I told Angel. "I don't."

Angel pushed into me, his thrusts bordering on violent. A powerful force took over when I said those words. It was like a weight had been lifted. He knew I didn't love Tyler anymore but with everything that had happened, he needed to be sure. He needed to hear me say it.

"Fucking right you don't." Angel brushed his nose up the length of my neck, a small smirk spreading on his lips. "You're mine, princess. Remember that the next time he kisses you."

CHAPTER NINE

Angel

I AM AN *asshole.*

I had no intention of fucking Jay. And that's what it was. Not making love. It wasn't sweet and caring. It was rough and violent. My dick was raw because of it.

With Jay sleeping peacefully beside me, I couldn't help but question why. Why was she still with me? Why did she accept my possessive ways? Why did God give her to me when she deserved so much better?

I kissed her shoulder, pulling her against my bare chest. The scent of sex and sweat wafted into my nose, forcing my heart to skip a beat. I didn't deserve her but I would make sure I showed her how much I needed her. Fuck everyone. Fuck Tyler and Charles. Fuck them all.

Jay and I deserved to be happy, and I would make damn sure that she remained happy with me.

A half an hour later, she stirred. "What time is it?"

"Time for us to get up," I grumbled.

"We should head back to your place." She sat up, stretched, and yawned. She smiled at me. Finally. It had been so long since I'd seen the smiles she gave reach her eyes.

I grabbed her hand, pulling her back into my arms and kissed her hard on the mouth. "I love you. I'm so fucking sorry. For everything. I know it's only words, but I *am* sorry. I'll show you with everything that I am how much I love you. How much I need you. And how much I want to marry you."

"We'll get through this." Her eyes shone. "I ..." She swallowed hard. "I'm ready to talk. About everything. The shit with Tyler." Her voice wavered. "Everything."

I sat up, pulling her between my legs and cupped her cheek. "I don't need to know the details with Tyler. I know he fucked you up. I get it. But I do need to know why you're scared."

"I'm not anymore." She sighed, her body relaxing. "I'm not. He really hurt me. He made these promises for years that no man would want me. That I wasn't good enough. He drilled it into my head that I guess I just started believing him. That's not fair to you, and I'm sorry."

"Don't be sorry," I kissed her softly on the mouth. "I know I'm jealous and possessive. I don't deserve you, but I will spend the rest of my life showing you just how much I appreciate you."

"It's funny." She crossed her legs under her. "I had to convince you in the beginning that there is such a thing as love and now, you've had to convince me that I can be happy."

"I'm not Tyler," I repeated the words I had said for weeks, but something was different about this time. After the kiss she shared with him, the closure she needed, saying the words now meant something more.

"I know …" Tears rolled down her cheeks. "I know that now."

"Good." I pulled her against me, wrapping my body around hers. "Good. That's … good. Anything else you need, I am here. Please know that."

"Just love me," she whispered. "That's all I need right now."

"I promise."

CHAPTER TEN

Jay

ANGEL HAD BEEN gone for a couple of hours before my body decided to wake. It had been a lazy morning, and I couldn't focus on anything but sleep. Waves of nausea had taken over every half an hour or so but they never forced me into the bathroom. I didn't know what was going on.

A moment of clarity struck.

Shit.

There was no way. No possible way.

I jumped from the bed when another wave hit me. Rushing to the bathroom, I fell to my knees almost missing the toilet. Spewing bile into the basin, the acidic burn made my eyes water.

GRIM

Fuck.

"Boss?"

"In here." Under normal circumstances, I would have given Creena shit for being in my room unannounced but right then, I didn't care.

"What's up?" she stopped at the door, frowning.

"I need you to do me a favor, and you can't tell anyone."

"Of course." She nodded for added effect. "What do you need?"

"Promise me," I pleaded. "Please."

"I promise."

Knowing I could trust her, I gave her a list of items to buy at the drug store and to hurry back. She didn't ask questions, didn't even ask for money.

My heart hurt with what the outcome of this situation could be. What if people found out and used that against us? Could people still see me as being president of a motorcycle club? To take me seriously? Too soon. These questions bouncing around in my mind were too much. I couldn't deal. I needed Angel.

***

(Angel)

It had been a stressful afternoon of dealing with Asher and his demons. Looked like we all had our own shit to deal with.

When the guys left, I headed to Jay's room at the back of the club. I needed some comfort that only she could provide.

"Jay?" I called out, stepping into the familiar space.

A muffled sound came from the bathroom.

"Princess?" I knocked lightly. "Are you in here?"

When no response came, I pushed open the door, finding Jay sitting on the floor. Several small boxes littered the area around her.

"Hey," I said gently. "What's going on?"

Her shoulders shook, a soft cry leaving her mouth.

Kneeling behind her, I wrapped my arms around her and kissed the side of her neck. "Talk to me."

She didn't say anything. She only held up a stick.

My eyes widened when I realized what she was holding. "What … um … Jay?"

She laughed, which came out more like a sob. "I'm sorry. I'm so fucking sorry."

"Sorry?" I turned her toward me, grabbing the stick from her hand. Two pink lines stared up at me. "Why are you sorry?" I still couldn't believe what I was looking at.

"Because …" Jay's chin quivered. "I don't know."

"Princess—" I kissed her softly on the mouth "—there is no reason to be sorry. It takes two and …" I looked down at the stick, noticing several more scattered beside her. All with pink lines, plus signs or words stating that she is pregnant. Pregnant. A baby. She was having my baby. "You're having my baby."

"I … oh, God." Her breath hitched. "I am. I'm pregnant. Angel, I'm pregnant." Her lips curled up into a smile.

"You're pregnant." My heart thumped, my stomach somersaulting.

Fucking A.

***

(Jay)

I wasn't sure why I thought it would be difficult to tell Angel that I was pregnant. After the countless bouts of nausea, it finally made sense as to why I hadn't been feeling well. The only thing I had to worry about was telling Max. My heart panged. It was hard for her to deal with being pregnant herself when she didn't have the support from the father. I liked Dale, but he needed to get his head out of his ass.

"What about Max?" I muttered, hot tears flowing down my cheeks. This emotional shit was annoying, and I was over it already. If I had to deal with this for nine months, it was going to drive me and everyone else insane.

Angel picked up the empty boxes, throwing them into the trashcan before helping me to my feet. He didn't answer, only held my hand and led me to the bed.

"Angel?"

"I love you," he said, kneeling between my legs. "You know, that right?"

"Of course, and I love you too."

"And Max loves you."

My eyes welled, my chest aching as if someone was squeezing my heart. But I didn't want to hurt Max. Her issues with Dale were hard to deal with. I wanted to be there for her, but I didn't want my pregnancy to come off as a slap in the face.

"I'm happy. I am so damn happy but I don't want … I want Max to love our baby and be there for it but I don't want any resentment."

"Jay …" Angel sighed, pulling me down onto his lap. "Max isn't like that. You know that she will love that baby like it's her own and when hers comes, our babies will grow up together. Be best friends and all that shit."

I laughed, wiping the tears from under my eyes. "I was so scared to tell you."

"Why?" he asked, taken aback.

"I don't know." I shrugged. "I know we have had our problems but I love you. I am so in love with you, and it makes me the happiest woman in the world to be carrying your baby."

"I never thought I could fall in love with you more." Angel cupped my cheek, staring intently into my eyes. "But I am. I am falling in love with you more and more each day."

My throat burned. "I love you. My King."

"I am proud to be your boyfriend, your fiancé, the father to your baby. Our baby." His eyes shone, glassing over with unshed tears.

"Our baby."

"And our little prince or princess will have so much love surrounding it, it will make all of the evil we are dealing with worth it."

"Everything will be worth it." I wrapped my arms around Angel, clinging onto him until all I felt was our love flowing around us.

I was pregnant.

I would never get used to the fact that I was carrying Angel Rodriguez's baby.

"I never thought I would say this—" his lips moved to the shell of my ear, his hot breath scorching the side of my face "—but you being pregnant with my baby makes me hard."

My eyes widened, a warmth settling deep in my belly.

His gaze had moved to my lower abdomen before he turned me in his arms. "Place your hands on the edge of the bed," his deep voice rumbled over me, sheltering me in a blanket of bliss. "I suggest holding on."

And I did.

For the rest of my life, I would … hold on.

*****THE END*****

Grab Rude (King's Harlots, #4):
https://www.aboutjmwalker.com/rude

ABOUT

J.M. Walker is an Amazon bestselling author who also hit USA Today with Wanted: An Outlaw Anthology. She loves all things books, pigs and lip gloss. She is happily married to the man who inspires all of her Heroes and continues to make her weak in the knees every single day.

"Above all, be the HEROINE of your own life..." ~ Nora Ephron

Website: http://www.aboutjmwalker.com/
Facebook: https://www.facebook.com/jm.walker.author
Reader Group: https://www.facebook.com/groups/JMsJems/
Twitter: https://twitter.com/jmwlkr
Instagram: https://www.instagram.com/jmwlkr/
Goodreads: https://www.goodreads.com/author/show/51 32169.J_M_Walker
BookBub: https://www.bookbub.com/authors/j-m-walker
Amazon: https://tinyurl.com/y7dpjkud
Newsletter: https://tinyurl.com/ya9hycak

Want more? Head on over to my website for my complete backlist!

https://www.aboutjmwalker.com/books